ALLAN AHLBERG
Grandma Fox

Illustrated by
ANDRÉ AMSTUTZ

PUFFIN BOOKS

PUFFIN BOOKS

Published by the Penguin Group: London, New York, Australia, Canada and New Zealand
Penguin Books Ltd, Registered Offices: Harmondsworth, Middlesex, England

Published in Puffin Books 2000
1 3 5 7 9 10 8 6 4 2

Printed in Hong Kong by Imago Publishing Ltd

A CIP catalogue record for this book is available from the British Library

ISBN 0–140–56402–0 Paperback

Fast Fox is hungry.
"I'd love a chicken sandwich," he says.

He looks in his kitchen.
Bread – yes!
Butter – yes!
Salt and pepper and
crisp green lettuce –
yes, yes, yes!

But *no* chicken.

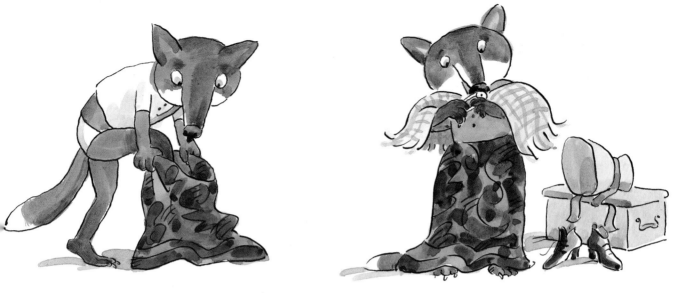

Fast Fox dresses up as a grandma
and sets off down the path.

Mother Hen is in the kitchen.
Slow Dog is reading the paper.
The chickens are playing in the yard.
Up comes Grandma.

"Oh, Grandma, what big eyes
you've got!" say the chickens.
"All the better to see you with,
my dears," says Grandma.

Mother Hen calls from the kitchen.
"Breakfast is on the table."
The chickens run inside.
"Drat it!" says Grandma.

Fast Fox
dresses up again.
He dresses up
as a doctor

and sets off down the path.

Mother Hen is in the kitchen.

Slow Dog is eating a biscuit.
The chickens are playing in the yard.
Up comes the doctor.

"Oh, Doctor, what big ears you've got!" say the chickens. "All the better to hear you with, my dears," says the doctor.

Mother Hen
calls from the kitchen.

"Lunch is on the table."
The chickens run inside.

"Dash it!" says the doctor.

Fast Fox dresses up *again*.
He dresses up as a postman

and sets off down the path.

Mother Hen is in
the kitchen.
Slow Dog is cleaning
the windows.

The chickens are playing
in the yard.
Up comes the postman.

"Oh, Postman, what a big bag you've got!" say the chickens.
"All the better," says the postman . . .

"to put

you in!”

Fast Fox runs off
with his bag of chickens.

Mother Hen calls from the kitchen.
"Supper is on the table."

"Supper is in the bag,"
thinks Fast Fox.
He jumps on his bike.

Fast Fox rides off.
Round the corner
of the house
he goes.

Then . . . bang!
Out of the blue sky
a big slow dog
falls on Fast Fox . . .

. . . and a bucket too.

So the story ends.
The chickens eat their supper.
Mother Hen makes a sandwich
for Slow Dog.

Fast Fox
makes a sandwich
for himself.
Bread – yes!
Butter – yes!
Salt and pepper and
crisp green lettuce –
yes, yes, yes!

But *no* chicken.

The End

FAST FOX, SLOW DOG

THE FAST FOX, SLOW DOG BOOKS

If you liked this story,
why not read another?
Try

Slow Dog's Nose

Sniff, sniff!
Slow Dog is on the trail.
Sniff, sniff!
His nose is in the air.
Sniff, sniff!
Something is cooking!

Oh no!
Those poor little chickens . . .

. . . who can save them?